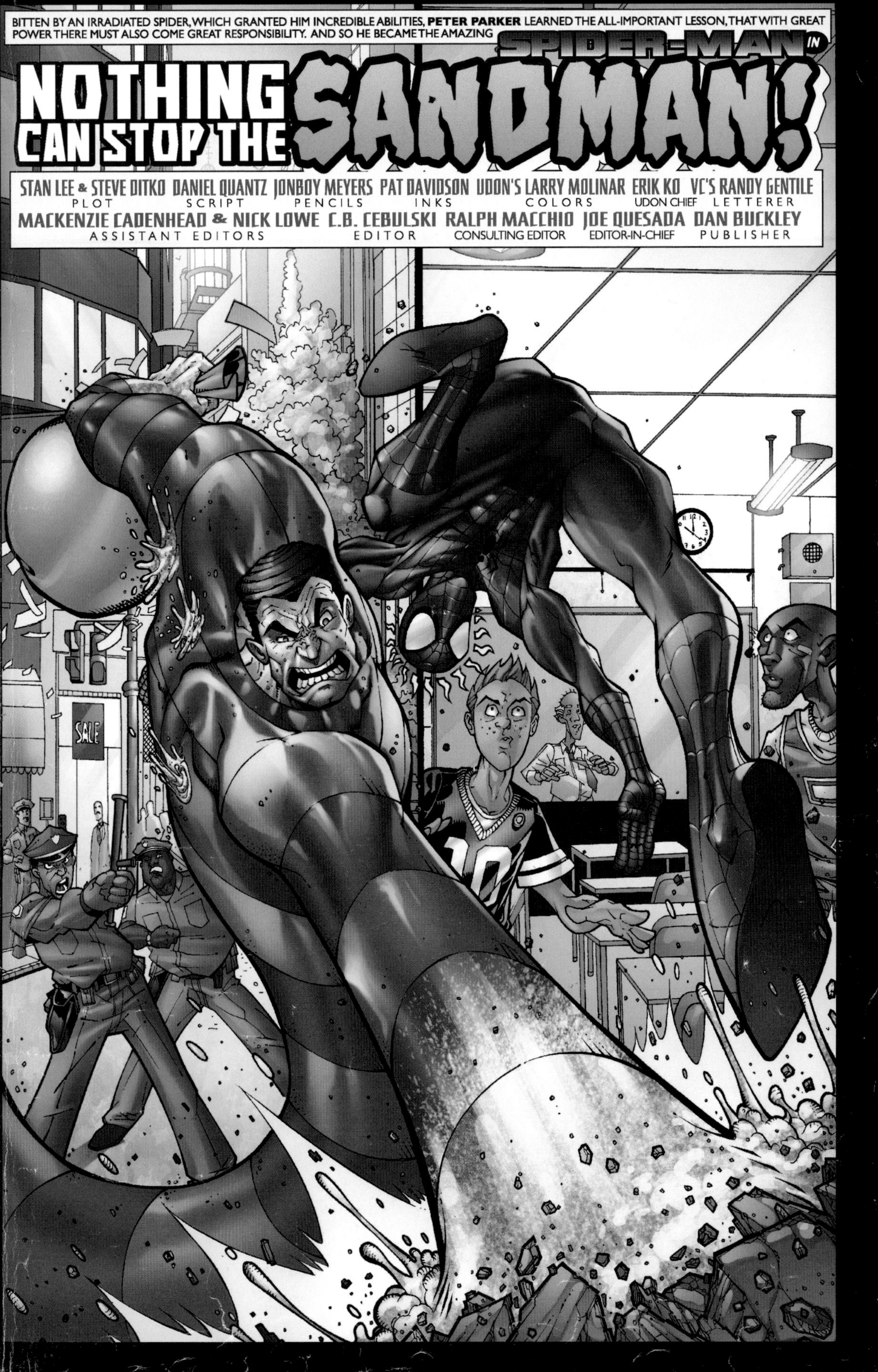
BITTEN BY AN IRRADIATED SPIDER, WHICH GRANTED HIM INCREDIBLE ABILITIES, PETER PARKER LEARNED THE ALL-IMPORTANT LESSON, THAT WITH GREAT POWER THERE MUST ALSO COME GREAT RESPONSIBILITY. AND SO HE BECAME THE AMAZING SPIDER-MAN IN
NOTHING CAN STOP THE SANDMAN!
STAN LEE & STEVE DITKO PLOT
DANIEL QUANTZ SCRIPT
JONBOY MEYERS PENCILS
PAT DAVIDSON INKS
UDON'S LARRY MOLINAR COLORS
ERIK KO UDON CHIEF
VC'S RANDY GENTILE LETTERER
MACKENZIE CADENHEAD & NICK LOWE ASSISTANT EDITORS
C.B. CEBULSKI EDITOR
RALPH MACCHIO CONSULTING EDITOR
JOE QUESADA EDITOR-IN-CHIEF
DAN BUCKLEY PUBLISHER
SALE
10

VISIT US AT

www.abdopub.com

Spotlight, a division of ABDO Publishing Company Inc., is the school and library distributor of the Marvel Entertainment books.

Library bound edition © 2006

Library of Congress Cataloging-in-Publication Data

Nothing Can Stop the Sandman!

ISBN 1-59961-016-7 (Reinforced Library Bound Edition)

All Spotlight books are reinforced library binding
and manufactured in the United States of America

Spotlight

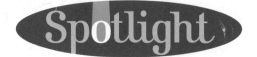

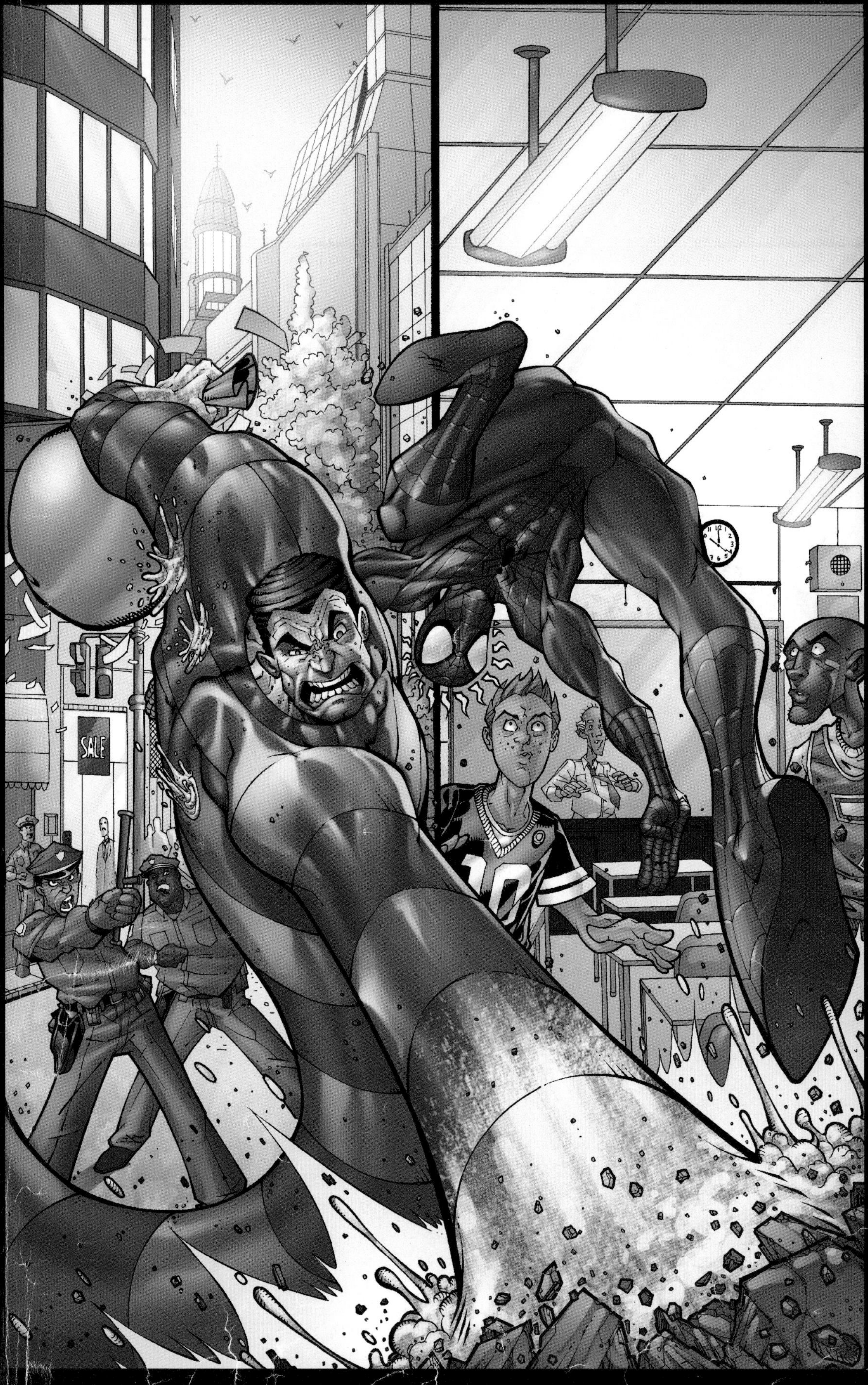
SALE

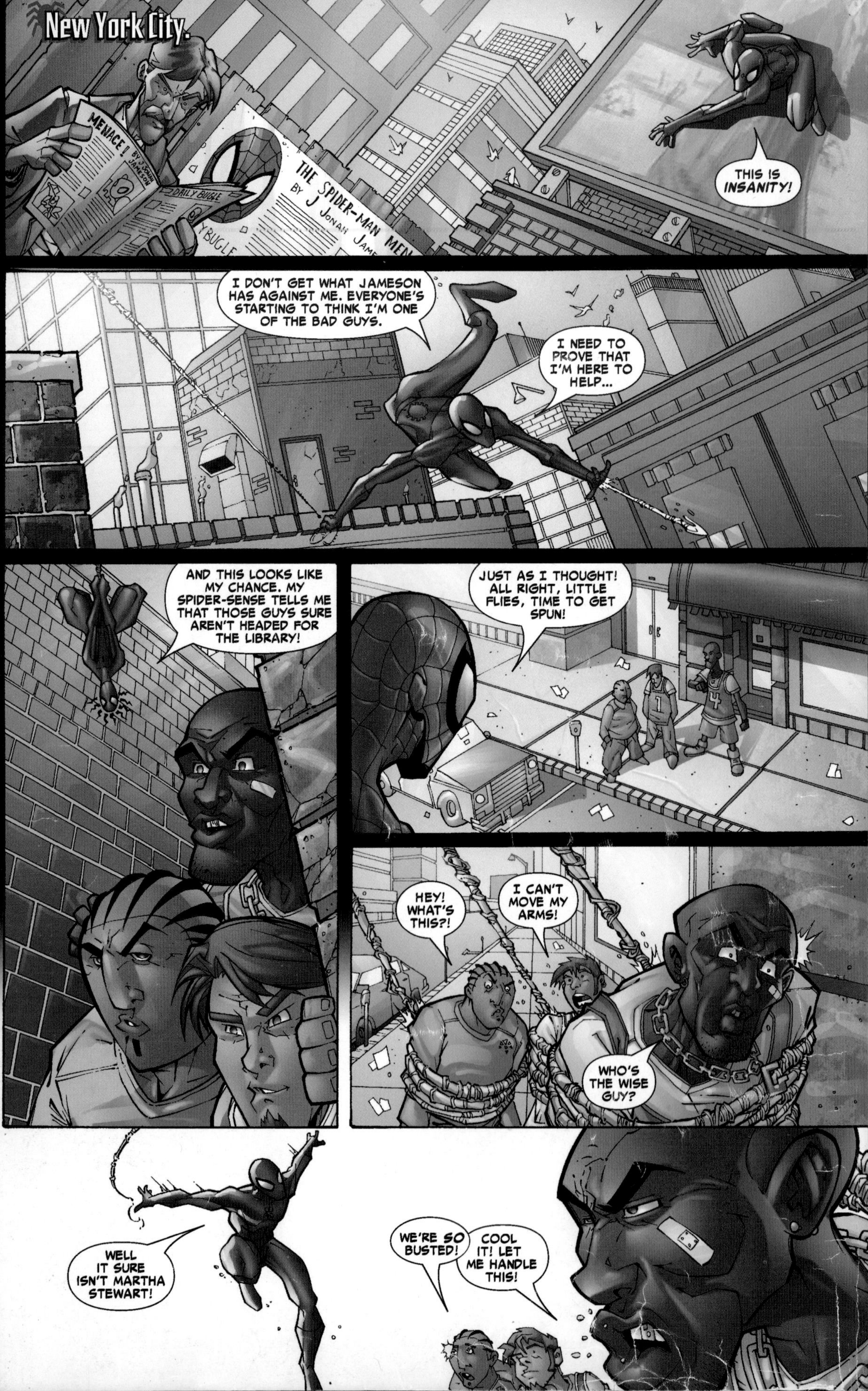
New York City.
MENACE! BY J JONAH JAMESON
DAILY BUGLE
THE SPIDER-MAN MEN
BY J JONAH JAME
THIS IS INSANITY!
I DON'T GET WHAT JAMESON HAS AGAINST ME. EVERYONE'S STARTING TO THINK I'M ONE OF THE BAD GUYS.
I NEED TO PROVE THAT I'M HERE TO HELP...
AND THIS LOOKS LIKE MY CHANCE. MY SPIDER-SENSE TELLS ME THAT THOSE GUYS SURE AREN'T HEADED FOR THE LIBRARY!
JUST AS I THOUGHT! ALL RIGHT, LITTLE FLIES, TIME TO GET SPUN!
HEY! WHAT'S THIS?!
I CAN'T MOVE MY ARMS!
WHO'S THE WISE GUY?
WELL IT SURE ISN'T MARTHA STEWART!
WE'RE SO BUSTED!
COOL IT! LET ME HANDLE THIS!

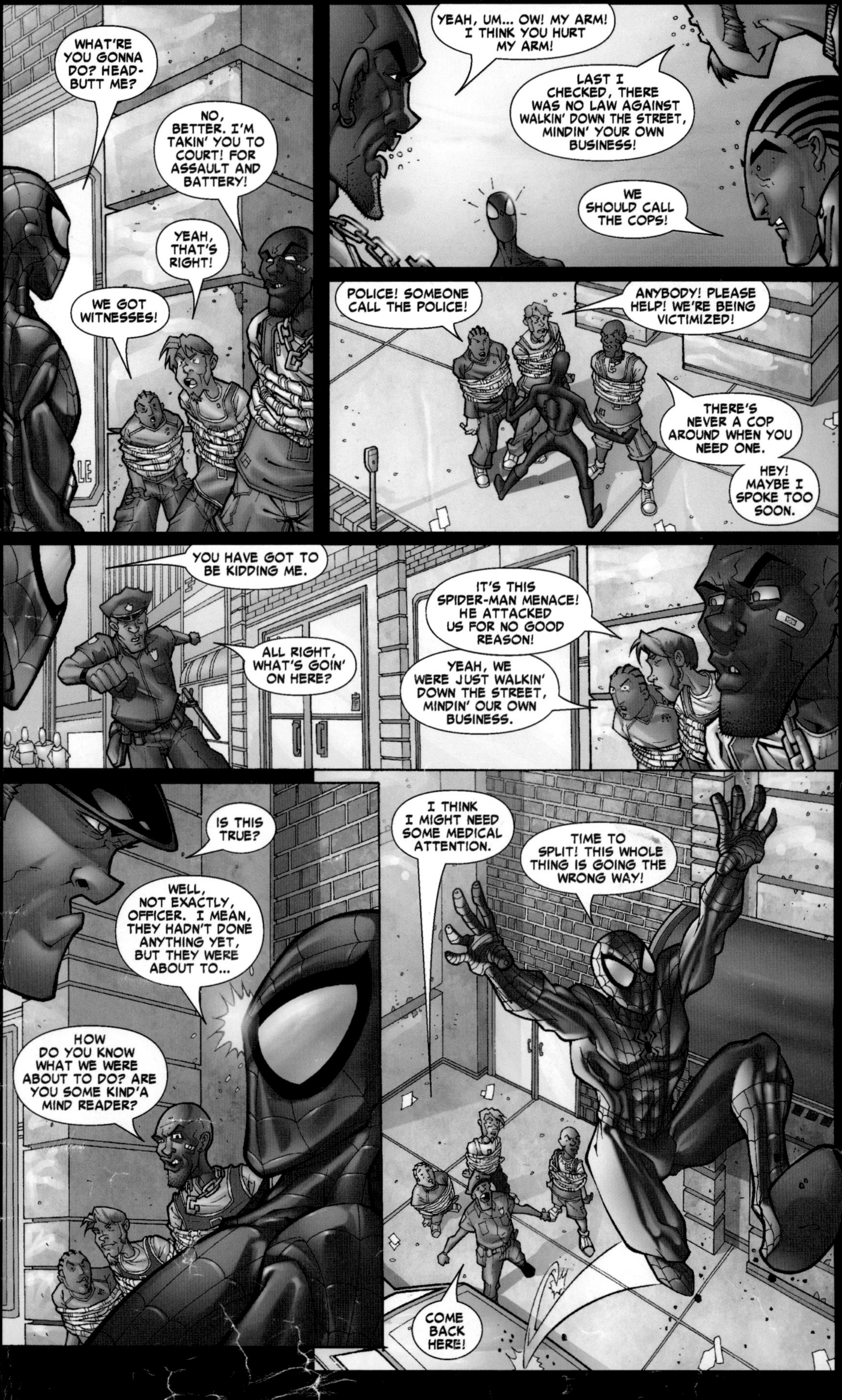
WHAT'RE YOU GONNA DO? HEAD-BUTT ME?
NO, BETTER. I'M TAKIN' YOU TO COURT! FOR ASSAULT AND BATTERY!
YEAH, THAT'S RIGHT!
WE GOT WITNESSES!
YEAH, UM... OW! MY ARM! I THINK YOU HURT MY ARM!
LAST I CHECKED, THERE WAS NO LAW AGAINST WALKIN' DOWN THE STREET, MINDIN' YOUR OWN BUSINESS!
WE SHOULD CALL THE COPS!
POLICE! SOMEONE CALL THE POLICE!
ANYBODY! PLEASE HELP! WE'RE BEING VICTIMIZED!
THERE'S NEVER A COP AROUND WHEN YOU NEED ONE.
HEY! MAYBE I SPOKE TOO SOON.
YOU HAVE GOT TO BE KIDDING ME.
ALL RIGHT, WHAT'S GOIN' ON HERE?
IT'S THIS SPIDER-MAN MENACE! HE ATTACKED US FOR NO GOOD REASON!
YEAH, WE WERE JUST WALKIN' DOWN THE STREET, MINDIN' OUR OWN BUSINESS.
IS THIS TRUE?
WELL, NOT EXACTLY, OFFICER. I MEAN, THEY HADN'T DONE ANYTHING YET, BUT THEY WERE ABOUT TO...
HOW DO YOU KNOW WHAT WE WERE ABOUT TO DO? ARE YOU SOME KIND'A MIND READER?
I THINK I MIGHT NEED SOME MEDICAL ATTENTION.
TIME TO SPLIT! THIS WHOLE THING IS GOING THE WRONG WAY!
COME BACK HERE!

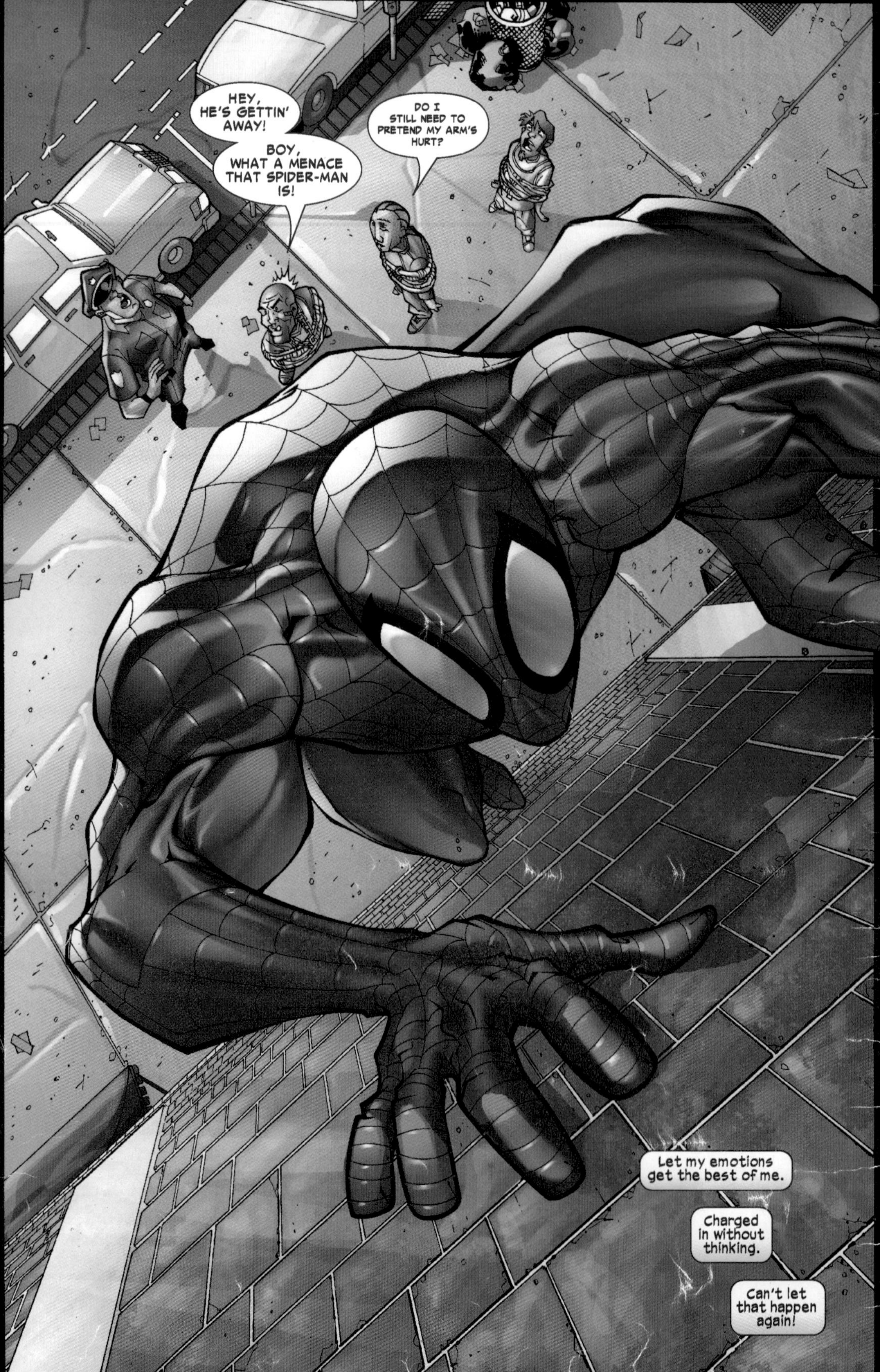
HEY, HE'S GETTIN' AWAY!
BOY, WHAT A MENACE THAT SPIDER-MAN IS!
DO I STILL NEED TO PRETEND MY ARM'S HURT?
Let my emotions get the best of me.
Charged in without thinking.
Can't let that happen again!

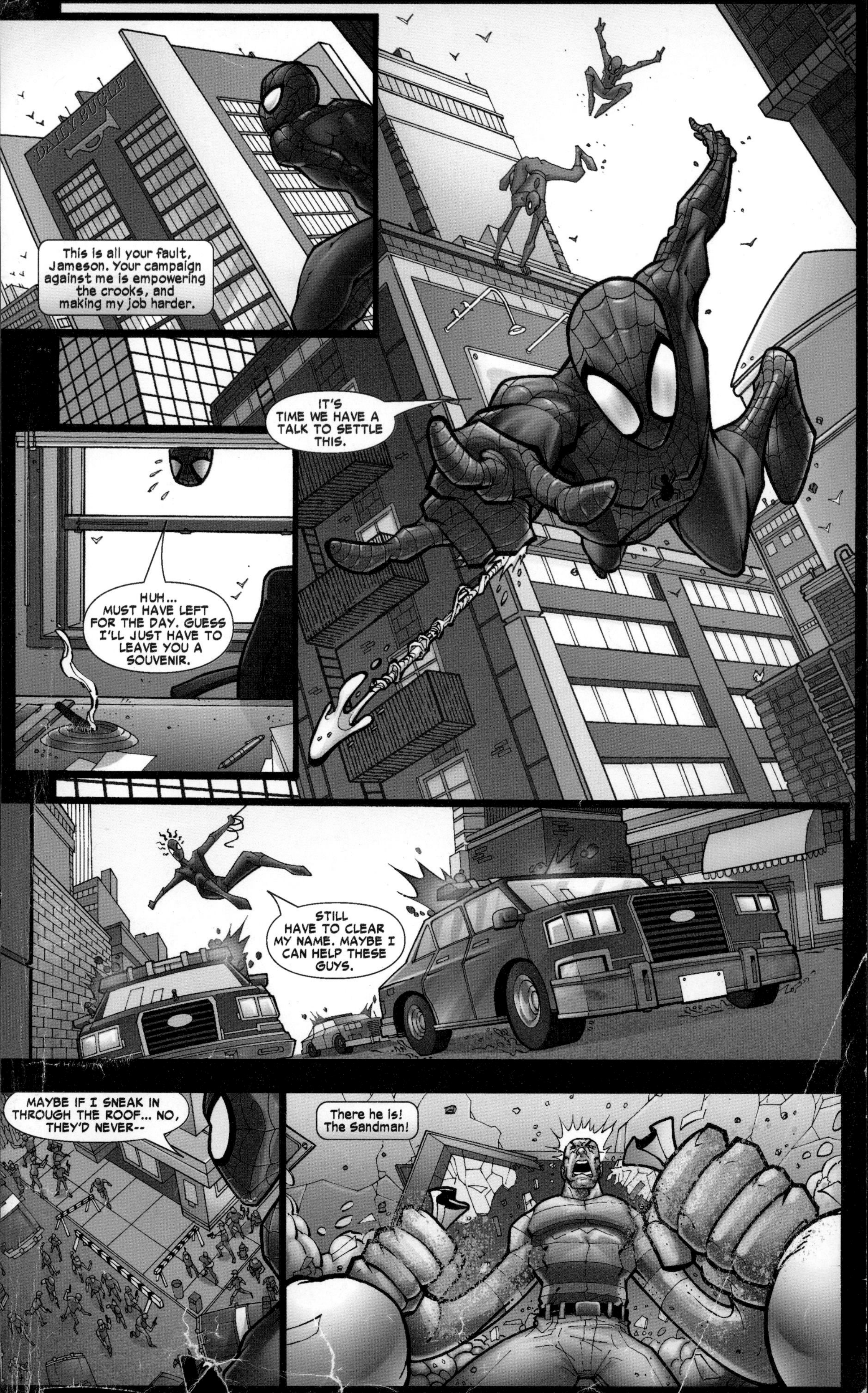
This is all your fault, Jameson. Your campaign against me is empowering the crooks, and making my job harder.
IT'S TIME WE HAVE A TALK TO SETTLE THIS.
HUH... MUST HAVE LEFT FOR THE DAY. GUESS I'LL JUST HAVE TO LEAVE YOU A SOUVENIR.
DAILY BUGLE
STILL HAVE TO CLEAR MY NAME. MAYBE I CAN HELP THESE GUYS.
MAYBE IF I SNEAK IN THROUGH THE ROOF... NO, THEY'D NEVER--
There he is! The Sandman!

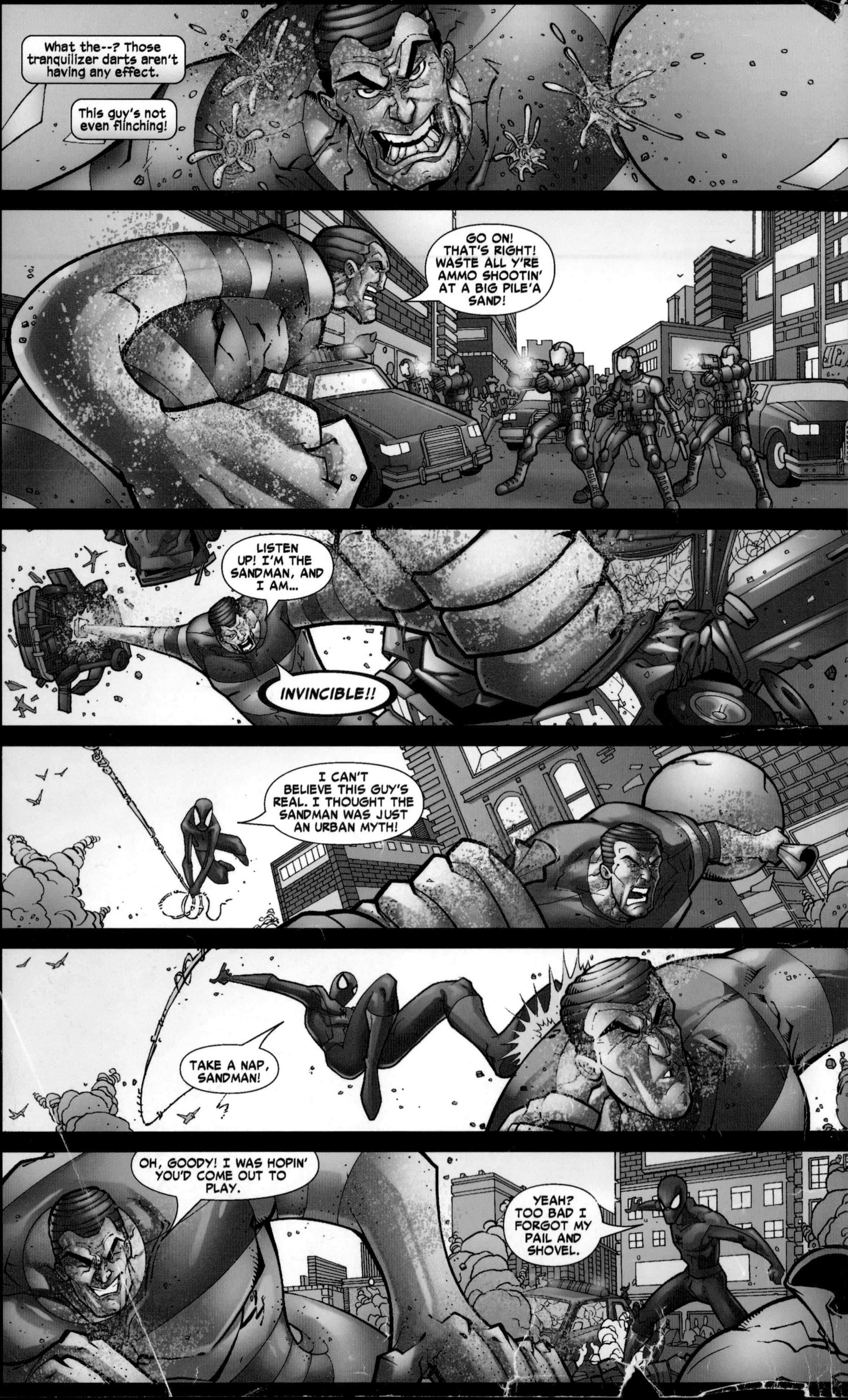
What the--? Those tranquilizer darts aren't having any effect.
This guy's not even flinching!
GO ON! THAT'S RIGHT! WASTE ALL Y'RE AMMO SHOOTIN' AT A BIG PILE'A SAND!
LISTEN UP! I'M THE SANDMAN, AND I AM...
INVINCIBLE!!
I CAN'T BELIEVE THIS GUY'S REAL. I THOUGHT THE SANDMAN WAS JUST AN URBAN MYTH!
TAKE A NAP, SANDMAN!
OH, GOODY! I WAS HOPIN' YOU'D COME OUT TO PLAY.
YEAH? TOO BAD I FORGOT MY PAIL AND SHOVEL.

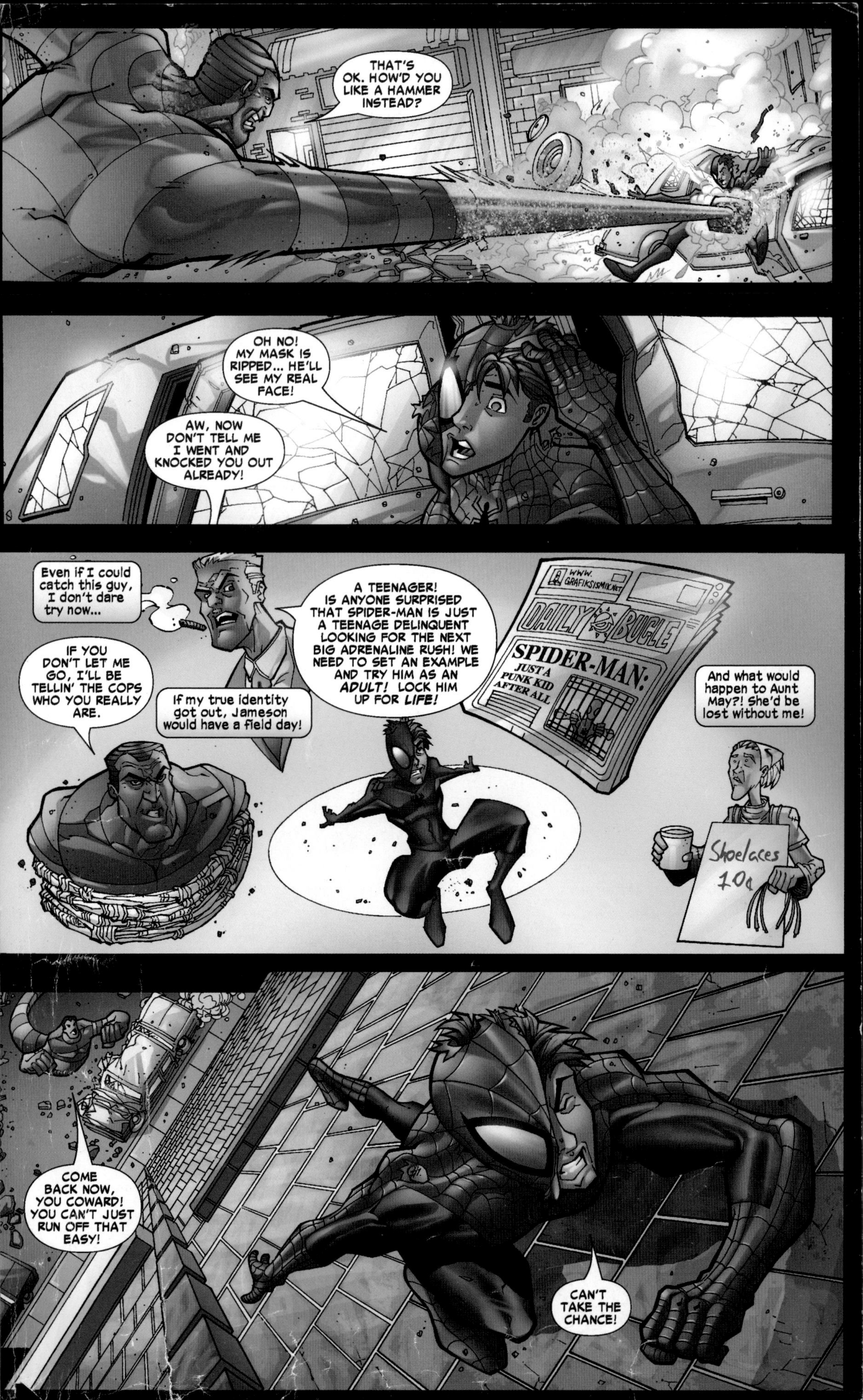
THAT'S OK. HOW'D YOU LIKE A HAMMER INSTEAD?
OH NO! MY MASK IS RIPPED... HE'LL SEE MY REAL FACE!
AW, NOW DON'T TELL ME I WENT AND KNOCKED YOU OUT ALREADY!
Even if I could catch this guy, I don't dare try now...
IF YOU DON'T LET ME GO, I'LL BE TELLIN' THE COPS WHO YOU REALLY ARE.
If my true identity got out, Jameson would have a field day!
A TEENAGER! IS ANYONE SURPRISED THAT SPIDER-MAN IS JUST A TEENAGE DELINQUENT LOOKING FOR THE NEXT BIG ADRENALINE RUSH! WE NEED TO SET AN EXAMPLE AND TRY HIM AS AN *ADULT!* LOCK HIM UP FOR *LIFE!*
WWW. GRAFIKSISMIC.NET
DAILY BUGLE
SPIDER-MAN: JUST A PUNK KID AFTER ALL
And what would happen to Aunt May?! She'd be lost without me!
Shoelaces 10¢
COME BACK NOW, YOU COWARD! YOU CAN'T JUST RUN OFF THAT EASY!
CAN'T TAKE THE CHANCE!

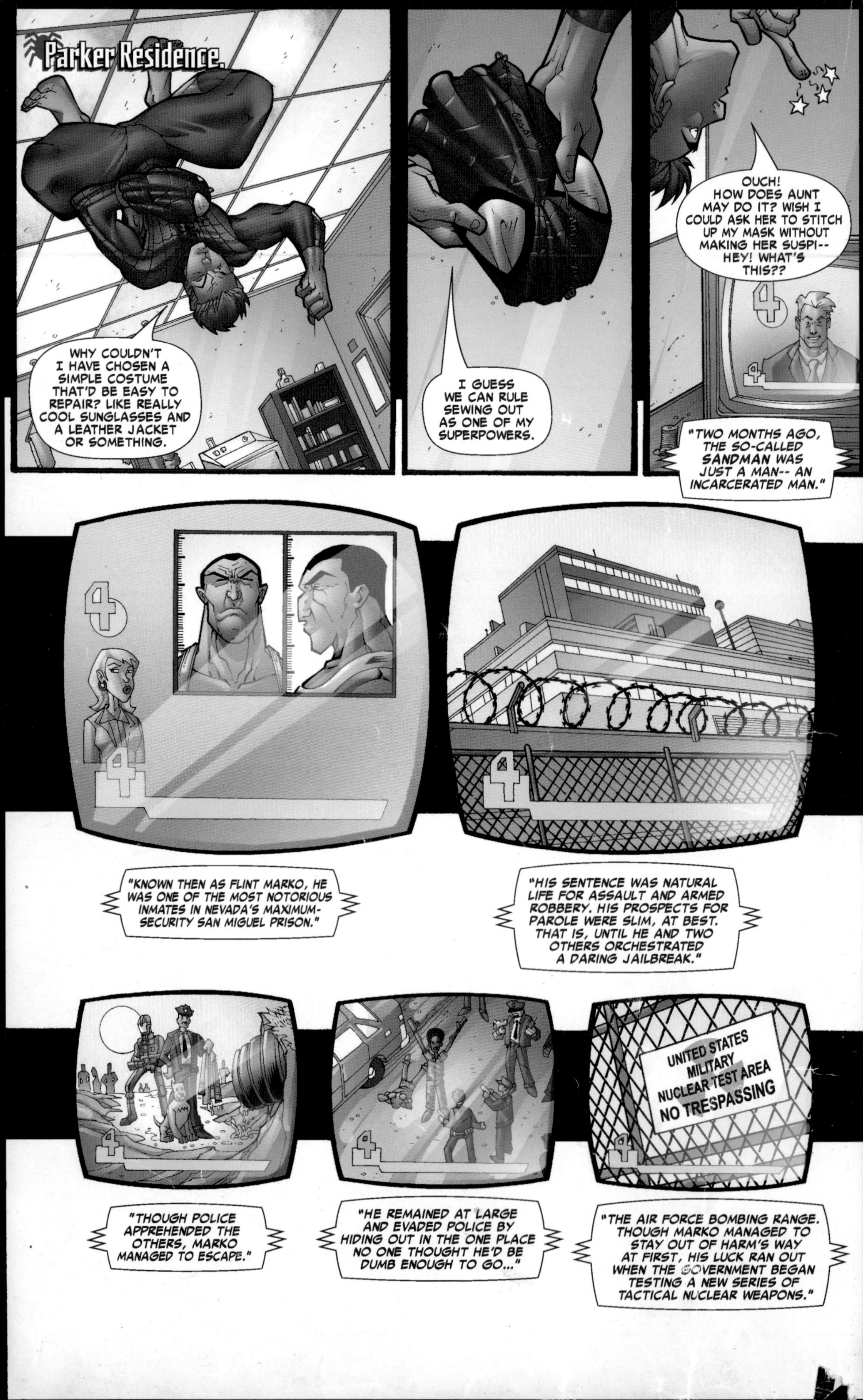
Parker Residence.
WHY COULDN'T I HAVE CHOSEN A SIMPLE COSTUME THAT'D BE EASY TO REPAIR? LIKE REALLY COOL SUNGLASSES AND A LEATHER JACKET OR SOMETHING.
I GUESS WE CAN RULE SEWING OUT AS ONE OF MY SUPERPOWERS.
OUCH! HOW DOES AUNT MAY DO IT? WISH I COULD ASK HER TO STITCH UP MY MASK WITHOUT MAKING HER SUSPI-- HEY! WHAT'S THIS??
"TWO MONTHS AGO, THE SO-CALLED SANDMAN WAS JUST A MAN-- AN INCARCERATED MAN."
"KNOWN THEN AS FLINT MARKO, HE WAS ONE OF THE MOST NOTORIOUS INMATES IN NEVADA'S MAXIMUM-SECURITY SAN MIGUEL PRISON."
"HIS SENTENCE WAS NATURAL LIFE FOR ASSAULT AND ARMED ROBBERY. HIS PROSPECTS FOR PAROLE WERE SLIM, AT BEST. THAT IS, UNTIL HE AND TWO OTHERS ORCHESTRATED A DARING JAILBREAK."
UNITED STATES MILITARY NUCLEAR TEST AREA NO TRESPASSING
"THOUGH POLICE APPREHENDED THE OTHERS, MARKO MANAGED TO ESCAPE."
"HE REMAINED AT LARGE AND EVADED POLICE BY HIDING OUT IN THE ONE PLACE NO ONE THOUGHT HE'D BE DUMB ENOUGH TO GO..."
"THE AIR FORCE BOMBING RANGE. THOUGH MARKO MANAGED TO STAY OUT OF HARM'S WAY AT FIRST, HIS LUCK RAN OUT WHEN THE GOVERNMENT BEGAN TESTING A NEW SERIES OF TACTICAL NUCLEAR WEAPONS."

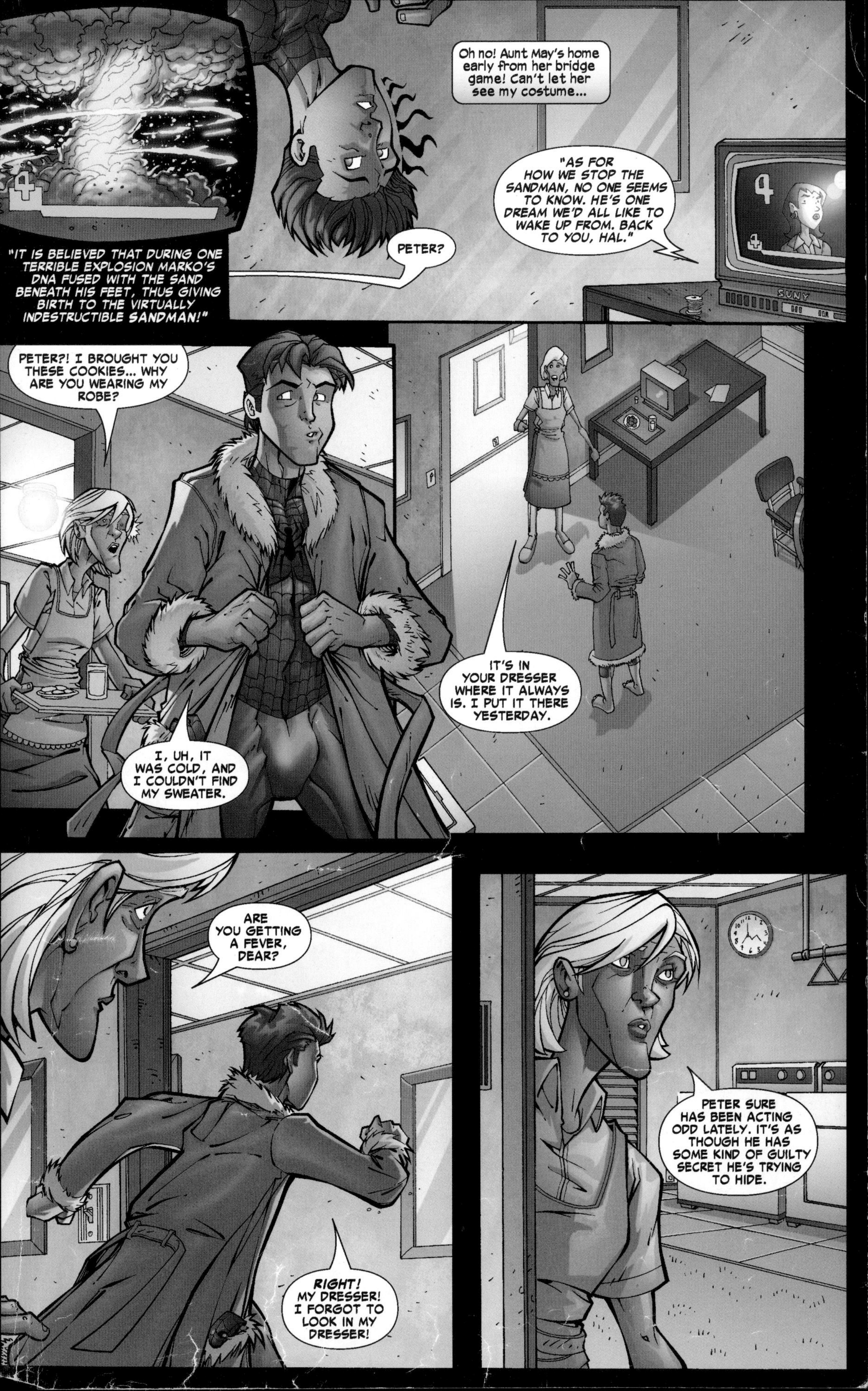
"IT IS BELIEVED THAT DURING ONE TERRIBLE EXPLOSION MARKO'S DNA FUSED WITH THE SAND BENEATH HIS FEET, THUS GIVING BIRTH TO THE VIRTUALLY INDESTRUCTIBLE SANDMAN!"
Oh no! Aunt May's home early from her bridge game! Can't let her see my costume...
"AS FOR HOW WE STOP THE SANDMAN, NO ONE SEEMS TO KNOW. HE'S ONE DREAM WE'D ALL LIKE TO WAKE UP FROM. BACK TO YOU, HAL."
PETER?
SUNY
PETER?! I BROUGHT YOU THESE COOKIES... WHY ARE YOU WEARING MY ROBE?
I, UH, IT WAS COLD, AND I COULDN'T FIND MY SWEATER.
IT'S IN YOUR DRESSER WHERE IT ALWAYS IS. I PUT IT THERE YESTERDAY.
ARE YOU GETTING A FEVER, DEAR?
RIGHT! MY DRESSER! I FORGOT TO LOOK IN MY DRESSER!
PETER SURE HAS BEEN ACTING ODD LATELY. IT'S AS THOUGH HE HAS SOME KIND OF GUILTY SECRET HE'S TRYING TO HIDE.

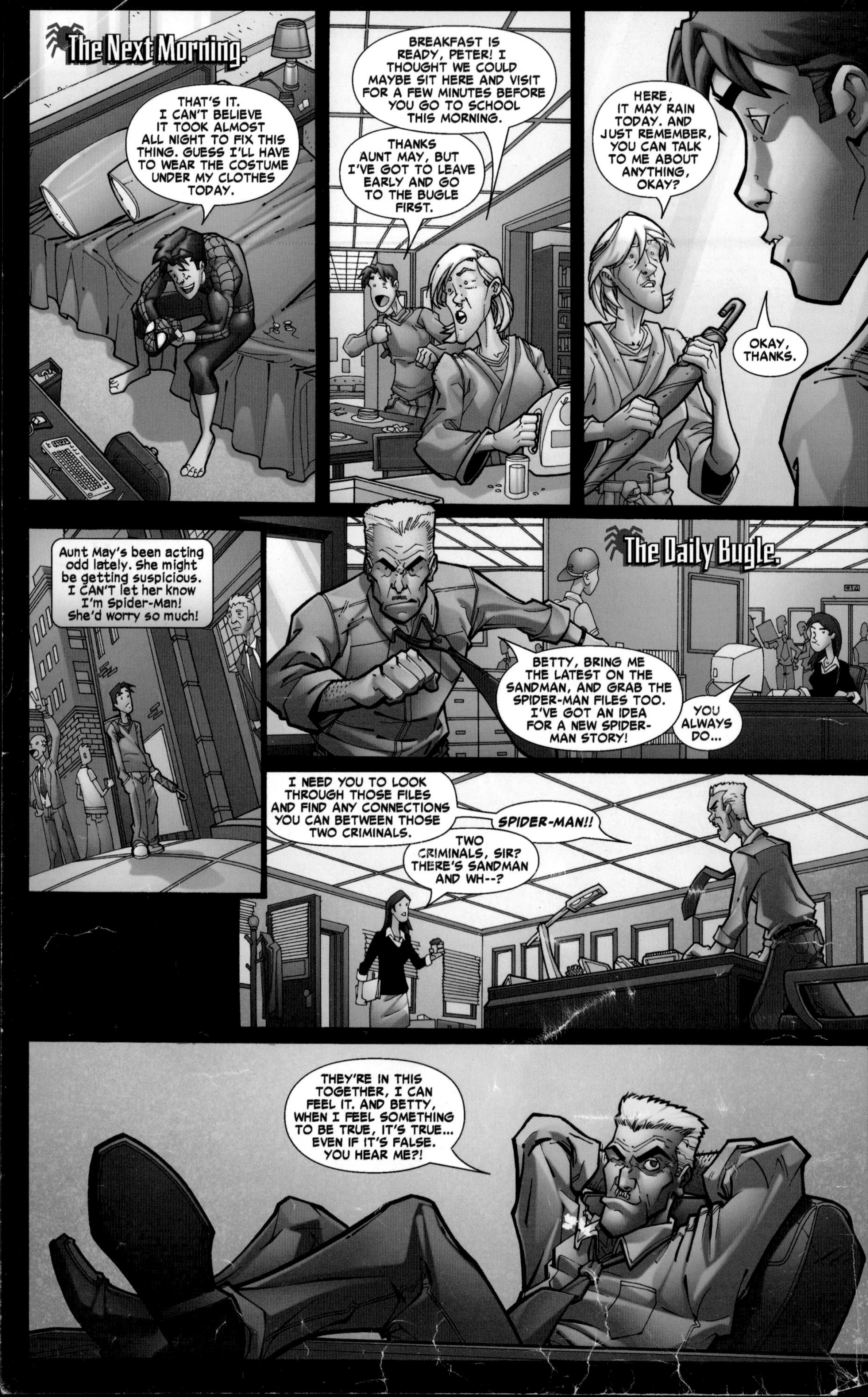
The Next Morning.
THAT'S IT. I CAN'T BELIEVE IT TOOK ALMOST ALL NIGHT TO FIX THIS THING. GUESS I'LL HAVE TO WEAR THE COSTUME UNDER MY CLOTHES TODAY.
BREAKFAST IS READY, PETER! I THOUGHT WE COULD MAYBE SIT HERE AND VISIT FOR A FEW MINUTES BEFORE YOU GO TO SCHOOL THIS MORNING.
THANKS AUNT MAY, BUT I'VE GOT TO LEAVE EARLY AND GO TO THE BUGLE FIRST.
HERE, IT MAY RAIN TODAY. AND JUST REMEMBER, YOU CAN TALK TO ME ABOUT ANYTHING, OKAY?
OKAY, THANKS.
Aunt May's been acting odd lately. She might be getting suspicious. I CAN'T let her know I'm Spider-Man! She'd worry so much!
The Daily Bugle.
BETTY, BRING ME THE LATEST ON THE SANDMAN, AND GRAB THE SPIDER-MAN FILES TOO. I'VE GOT AN IDEA FOR A NEW SPIDER-MAN STORY!
YOU ALWAYS DO...
I NEED YOU TO LOOK THROUGH THOSE FILES AND FIND ANY CONNECTIONS YOU CAN BETWEEN THOSE TWO CRIMINALS.
TWO CRIMINALS, SIR? THERE'S SANDMAN AND WH--?
SPIDER-MAN!!
THEY'RE IN THIS TOGETHER, I CAN FEEL IT. AND BETTY, WHEN I FEEL SOMETHING TO BE TRUE, IT'S TRUE... EVEN IF IT'S FALSE. YOU HEAR ME?!

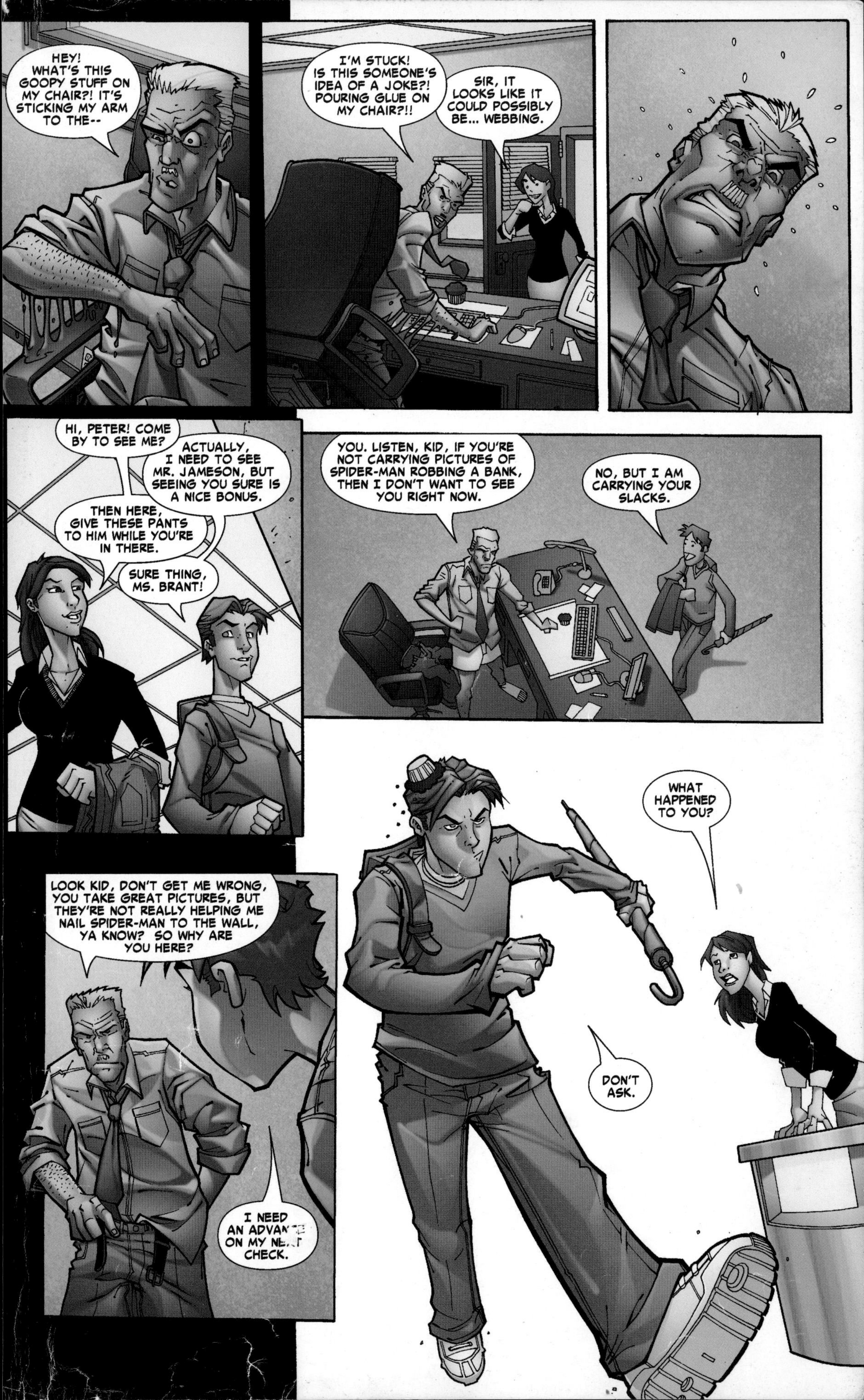
HEY! WHAT'S THIS GOOPY STUFF ON MY CHAIR?! IT'S STICKING MY ARM TO THE--
I'M STUCK! IS THIS SOMEONE'S IDEA OF A JOKE?! POURING GLUE ON MY CHAIR?!!
SIR, IT LOOKS LIKE IT COULD POSSIBLY BE... WEBBING.
HI, PETER! COME BY TO SEE ME?
ACTUALLY, I NEED TO SEE MR. JAMESON, BUT SEEING YOU SURE IS A NICE BONUS.
THEN HERE, GIVE THESE PANTS TO HIM WHILE YOU'RE IN THERE.
SURE THING, MS. BRANT!
YOU. LISTEN, KID, IF YOU'RE NOT CARRYING PICTURES OF SPIDER-MAN ROBBING A BANK, THEN I DON'T WANT TO SEE YOU RIGHT NOW.
NO, BUT I AM CARRYING YOUR SLACKS.
LOOK KID, DON'T GET ME WRONG, YOU TAKE GREAT PICTURES, BUT THEY'RE NOT REALLY HELPING ME NAIL SPIDER-MAN TO THE WALL, YA KNOW? SO WHY ARE YOU HERE?
I NEED AN ADVANCE ON MY NEXT CHECK.
WHAT HAPPENED TO YOU?
DON'T ASK.

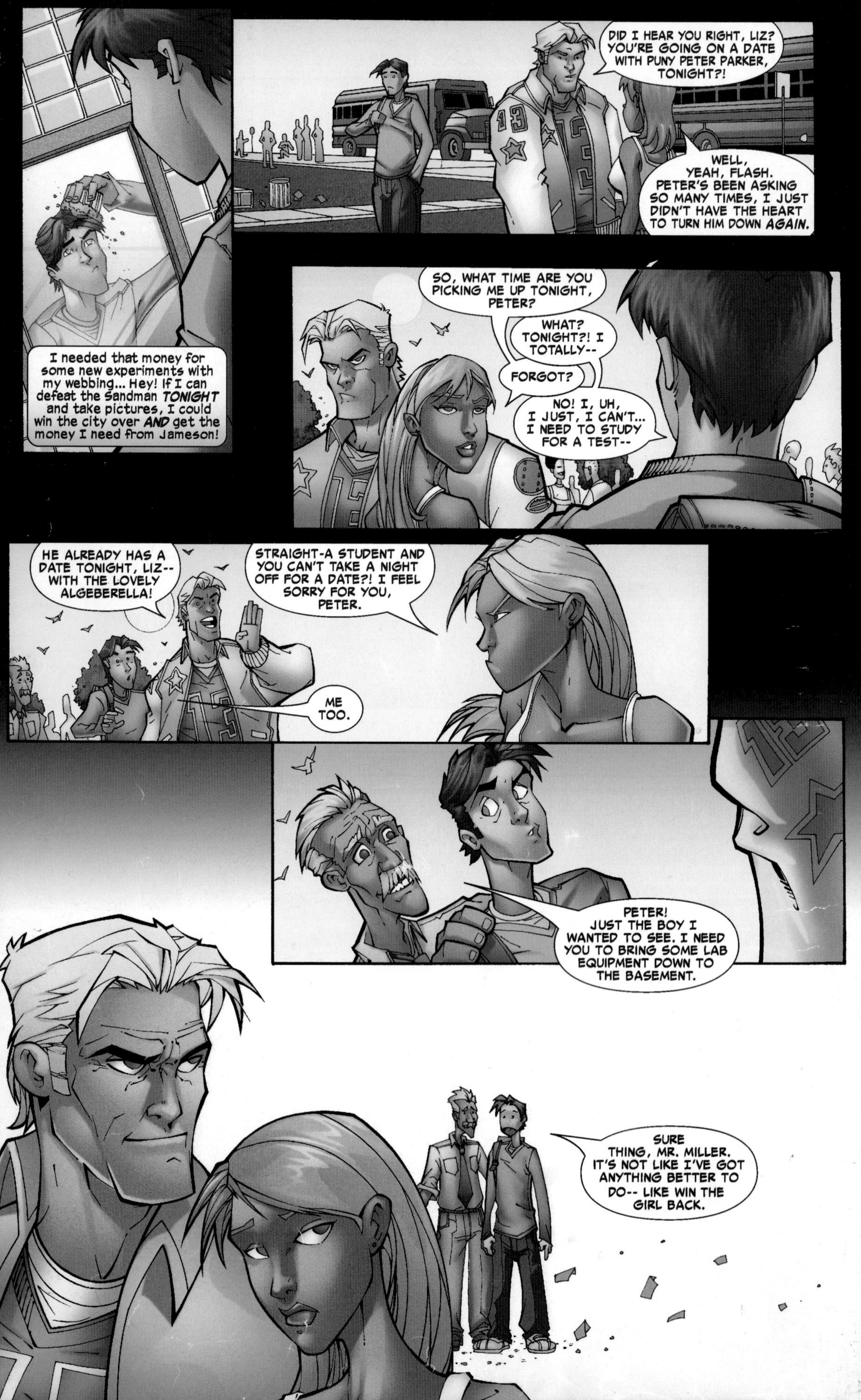
I needed that money for some new experiments with my webbing... Hey! If I can defeat the Sandman TONIGHT and take pictures, I could win the city over AND get the money I need from Jameson!
DID I HEAR YOU RIGHT, LIZ? YOU'RE GOING ON A DATE WITH PUNY PETER PARKER, TONIGHT?!
WELL, YEAH, FLASH. PETER'S BEEN ASKING SO MANY TIMES, I JUST DIDN'T HAVE THE HEART TO TURN HIM DOWN AGAIN.
SO, WHAT TIME ARE YOU PICKING ME UP TONIGHT, PETER?
WHAT? TONIGHT?! I TOTALLY--
FORGOT?
NO! I, UH, I JUST, I CAN'T... I NEED TO STUDY FOR A TEST--
HE ALREADY HAS A DATE TONIGHT, LIZ-- WITH THE LOVELY ALGEBERELLA!
STRAIGHT-A STUDENT AND YOU CAN'T TAKE A NIGHT OFF FOR A DATE?! I FEEL SORRY FOR YOU, PETER.
ME TOO.
PETER! JUST THE BOY I WANTED TO SEE. I NEED YOU TO BRING SOME LAB EQUIPMENT DOWN TO THE BASEMENT.
SURE THING, MR. MILLER. IT'S NOT LIKE I'VE GOT ANYTHING BETTER TO DO-- LIKE WIN THE GIRL BACK.

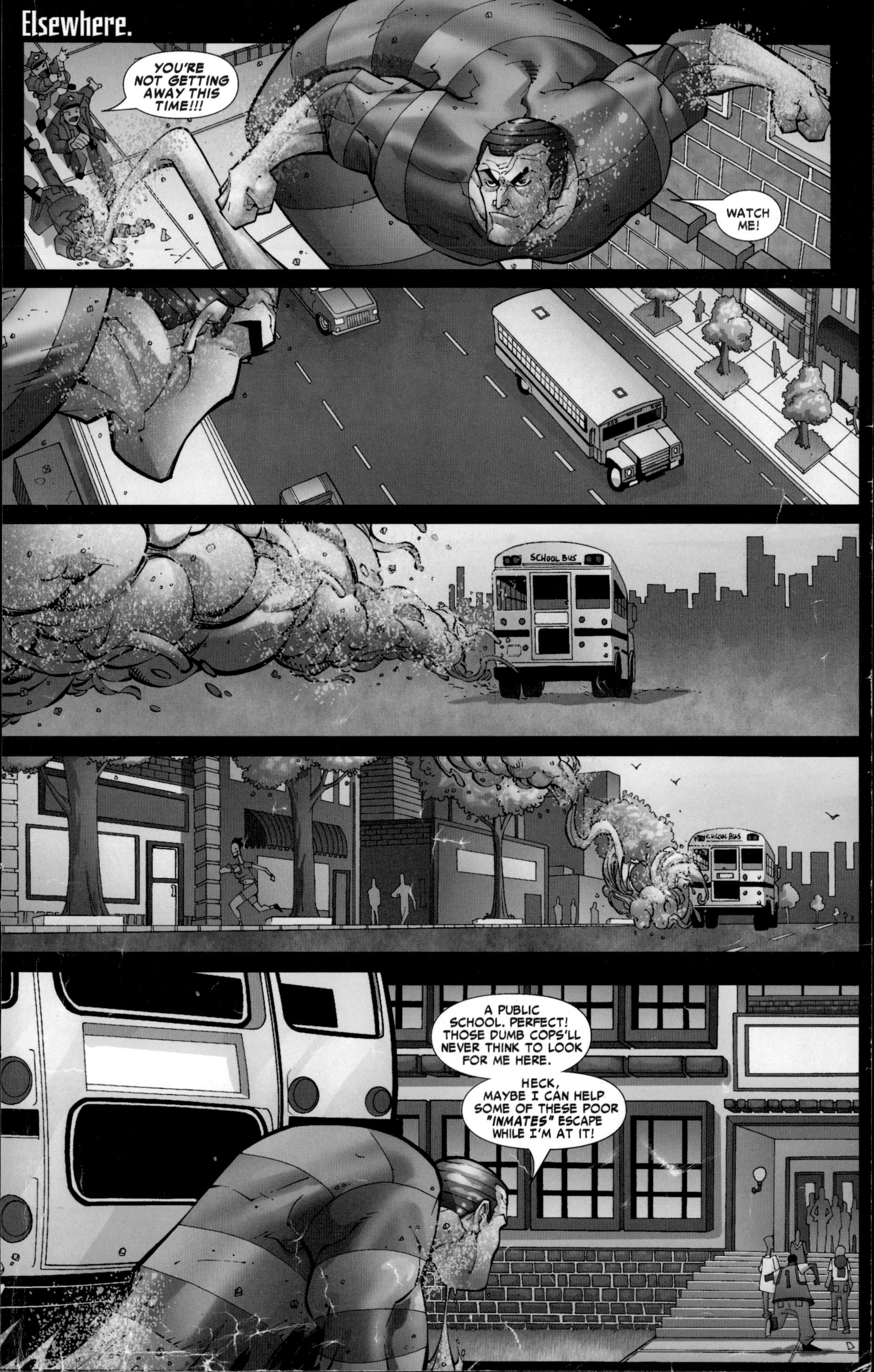
Elsewhere.
YOU'RE NOT GETTING AWAY THIS TIME!!!
WATCH ME!
SCHOOL BUS
SCHOOL BUS
A PUBLIC SCHOOL. PERFECT! THOSE DUMB COPS'LL NEVER THINK TO LOOK FOR ME HERE.
HECK, MAYBE I CAN HELP SOME OF THESE POOR "INMATES" ESCAPE WHILE I'M AT IT!

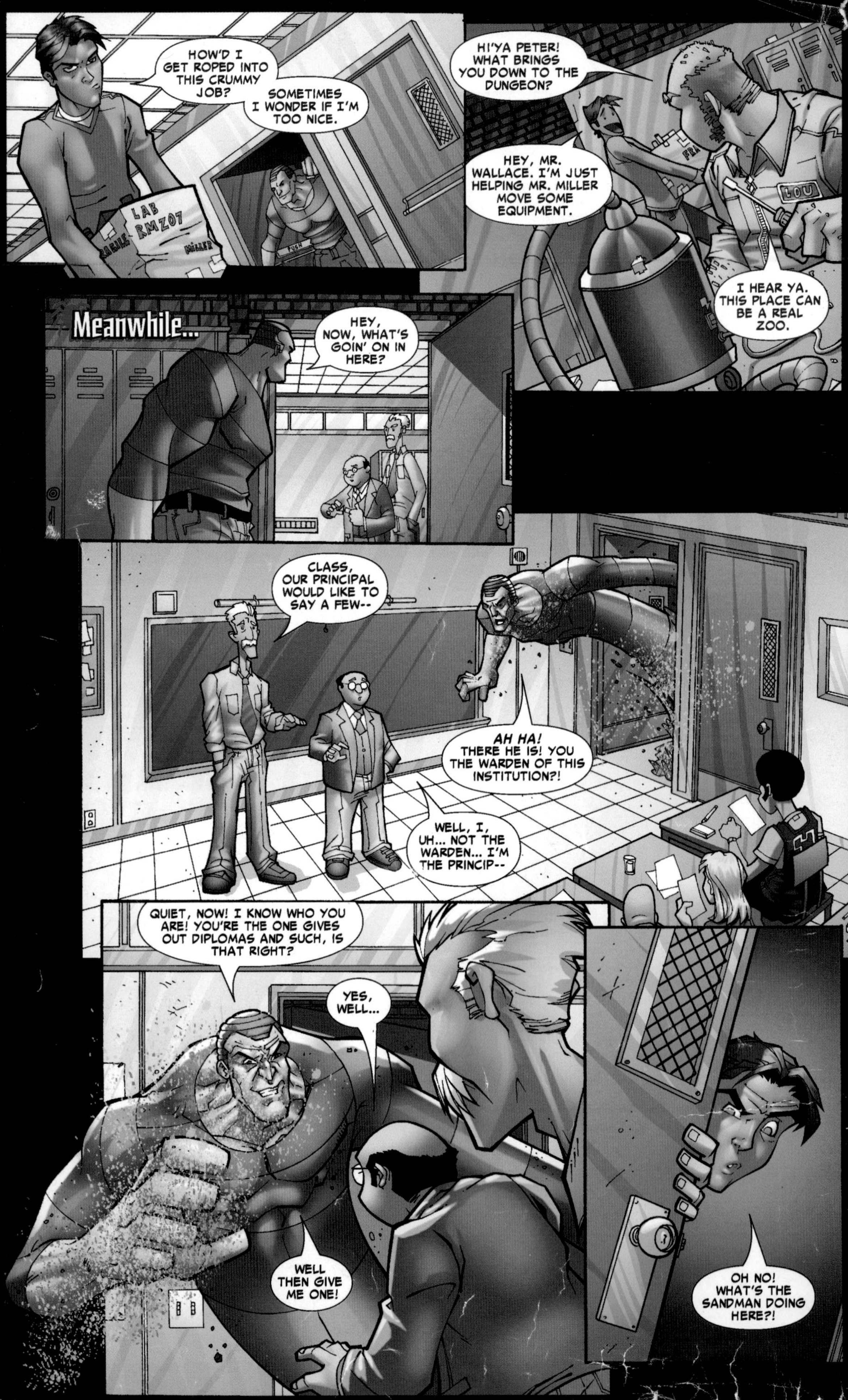
HOW'D I GET ROPED INTO THIS CRUMMY JOB?
SOMETIMES I WONDER IF I'M TOO NICE.
LAB RM207
MILLER
PUSH
HI'YA PETER! WHAT BRINGS YOU DOWN TO THE DUNGEON?
HEY, MR. WALLACE. I'M JUST HELPING MR. MILLER MOVE SOME EQUIPMENT.
LOU
I HEAR YA. THIS PLACE CAN BE A REAL ZOO.
Meanwhile...
HEY, NOW, WHAT'S GOIN' ON IN HERE?
CLASS, OUR PRINCIPAL WOULD LIKE TO SAY A FEW--
AH HA! THERE HE IS! YOU THE WARDEN OF THIS INSTITUTION?!
WELL, I, UH... NOT THE WARDEN... I'M THE PRINCIP--
QUIET, NOW! I KNOW WHO YOU ARE! YOU'RE THE ONE GIVES OUT DIPLOMAS AND SUCH, IS THAT RIGHT?
YES, WELL...
WELL THEN GIVE ME ONE!
OH NO! WHAT'S THE SANDMAN DOING HERE?!

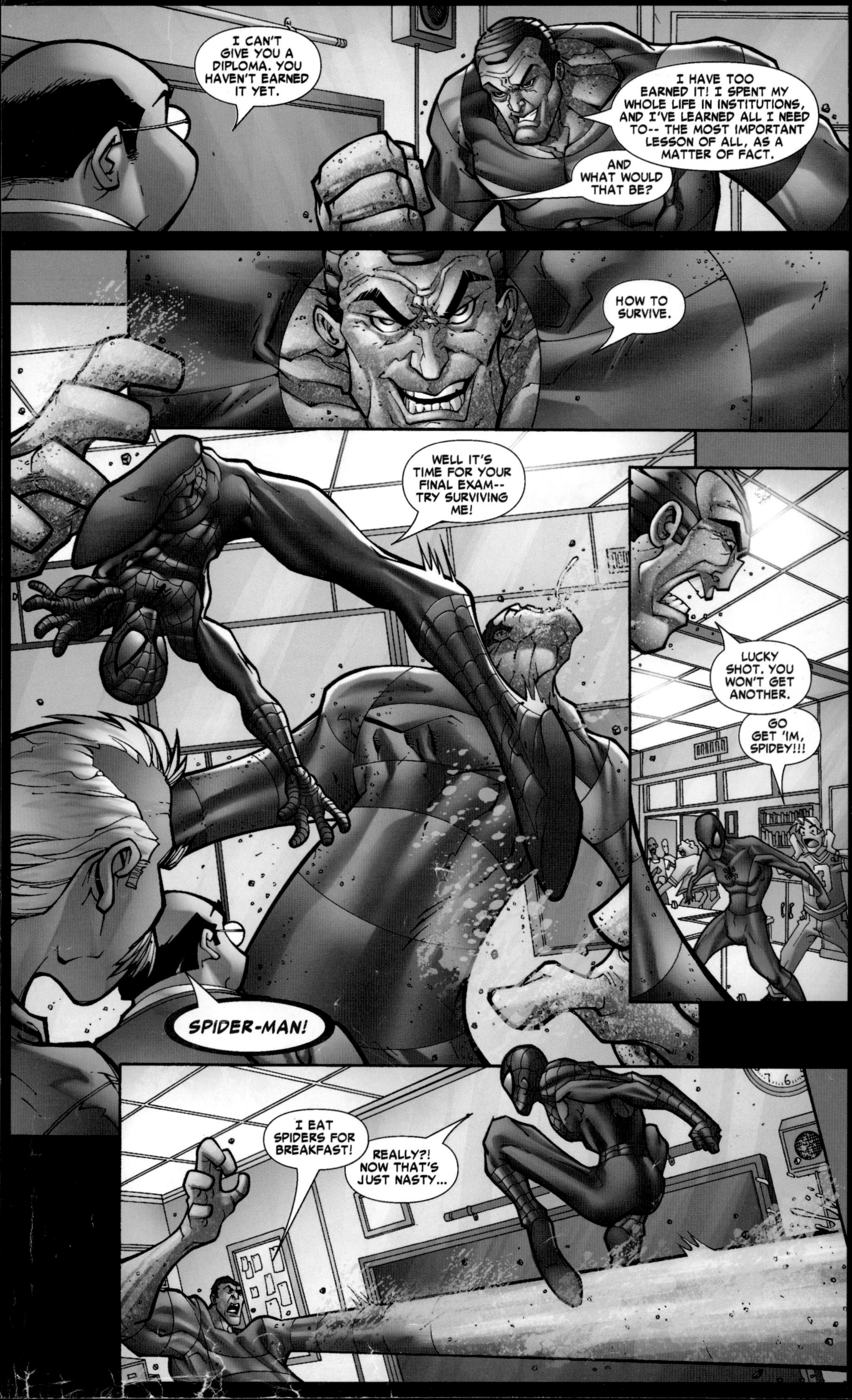
I CAN'T GIVE YOU A DIPLOMA. YOU HAVEN'T EARNED IT YET.
I HAVE TOO EARNED IT! I SPENT MY WHOLE LIFE IN INSTITUTIONS, AND I'VE LEARNED ALL I NEED TO-- THE MOST IMPORTANT LESSON OF ALL, AS A MATTER OF FACT.
AND WHAT WOULD THAT BE?
HOW TO SURVIVE.
WELL IT'S TIME FOR YOUR FINAL EXAM-- TRY SURVIVING ME!
SPIDER-MAN!
LUCKY SHOT. YOU WON'T GET ANOTHER.
GO GET 'IM, SPIDEY!!!
I EAT SPIDERS FOR BREAKFAST!
REALLY?! NOW THAT'S JUST NASTY...

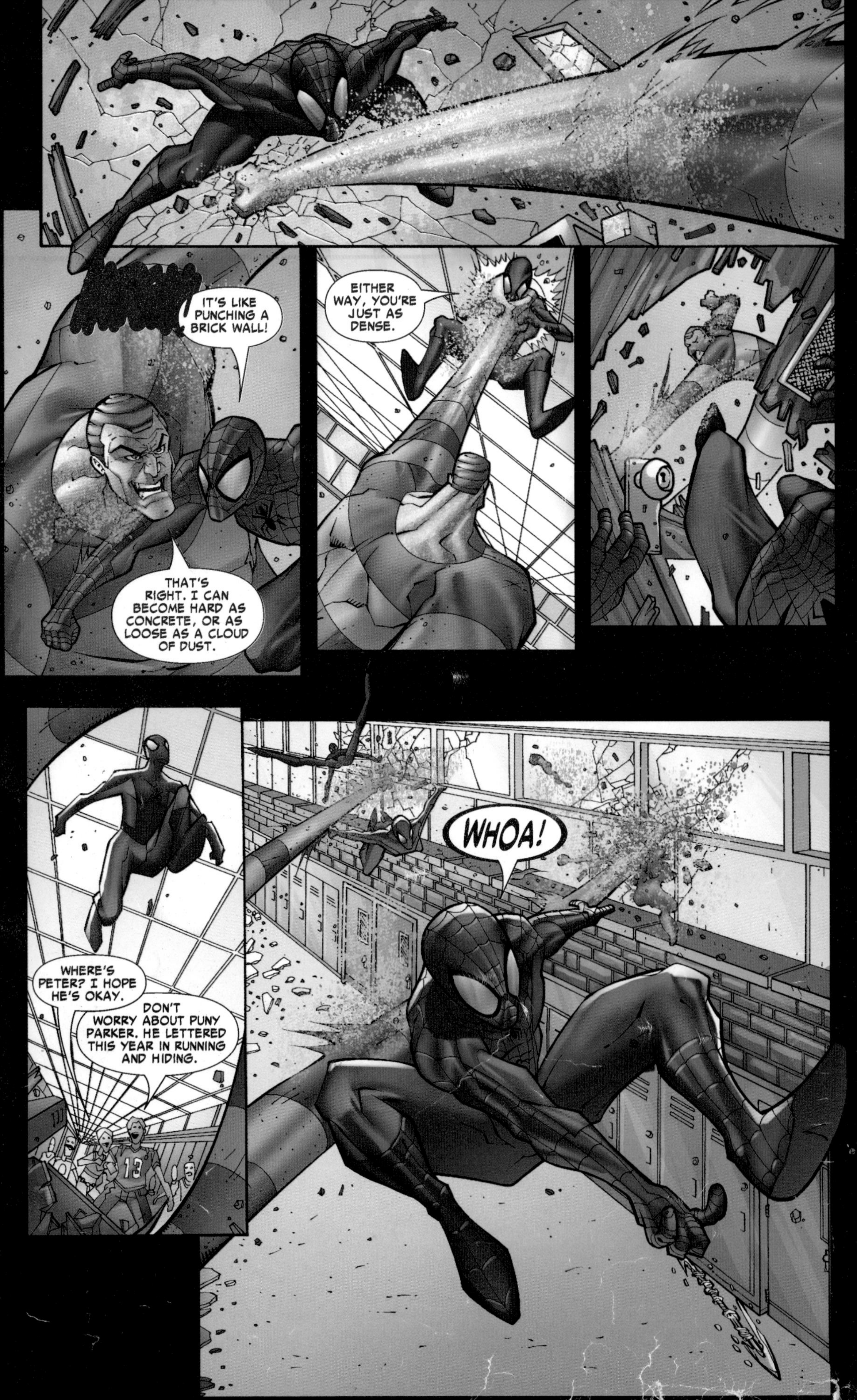
IT'S LIKE PUNCHING A BRICK WALL!
THAT'S RIGHT. I CAN BECOME HARD AS CONCRETE, OR AS LOOSE AS A CLOUD OF DUST.
EITHER WAY, YOU'RE JUST AS DENSE.
WHERE'S PETER? I HOPE HE'S OKAY.
DON'T WORRY ABOUT PUNY PARKER. HE LETTERED THIS YEAR IN RUNNING AND HIDING.
WHOA!

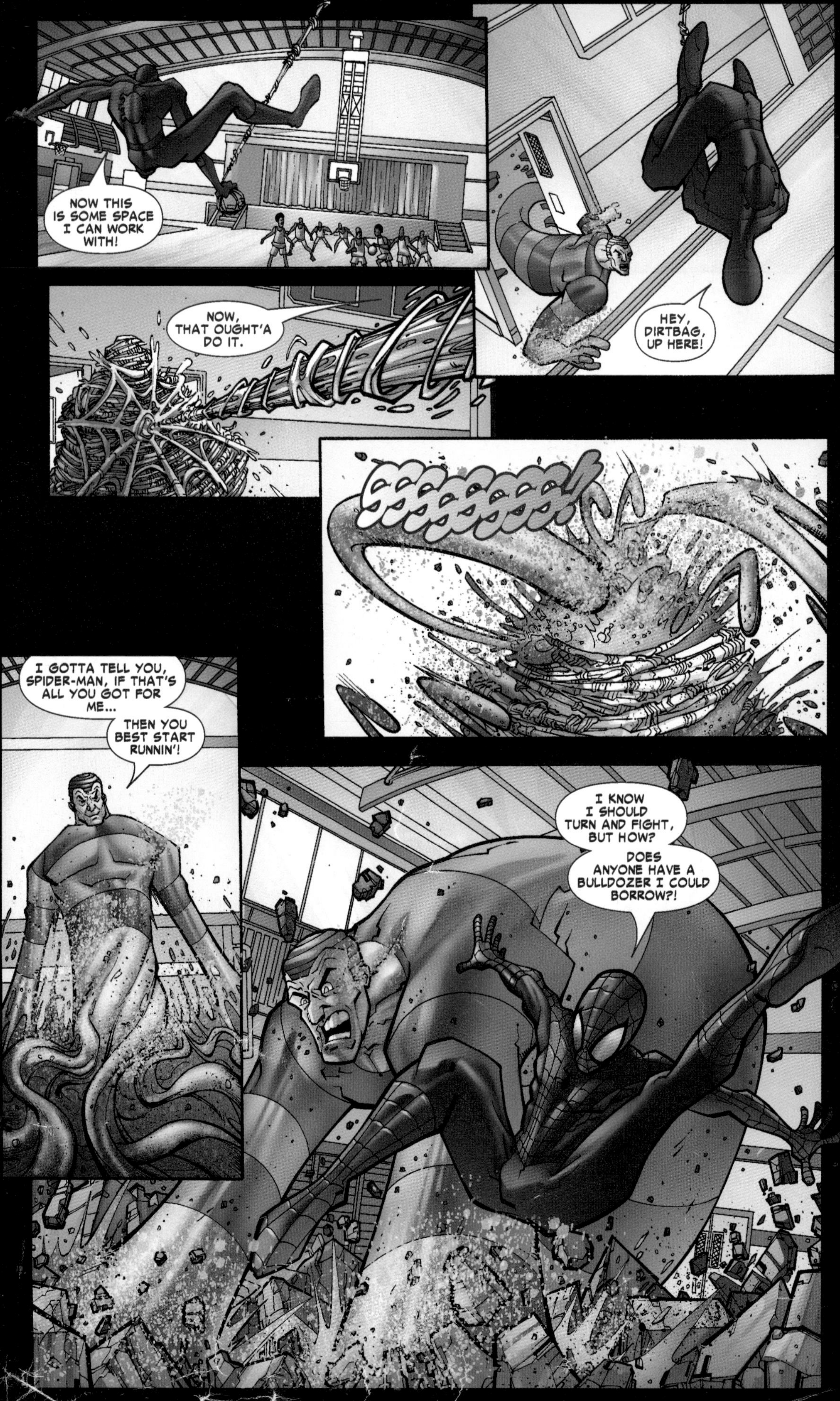
NOW THIS IS SOME SPACE I CAN WORK WITH!
HEY, DIRTBAG, UP HERE!
NOW, THAT OUGHT'A DO IT.
SSSSSSSS!
I GOTTA TELL YOU, SPIDER-MAN, IF THAT'S ALL YOU GOT FOR ME...
THEN YOU BEST START RUNNIN'!
I KNOW I SHOULD TURN AND FIGHT, BUT HOW?
DOES ANYONE HAVE A BULLDOZER I COULD BORROW?!

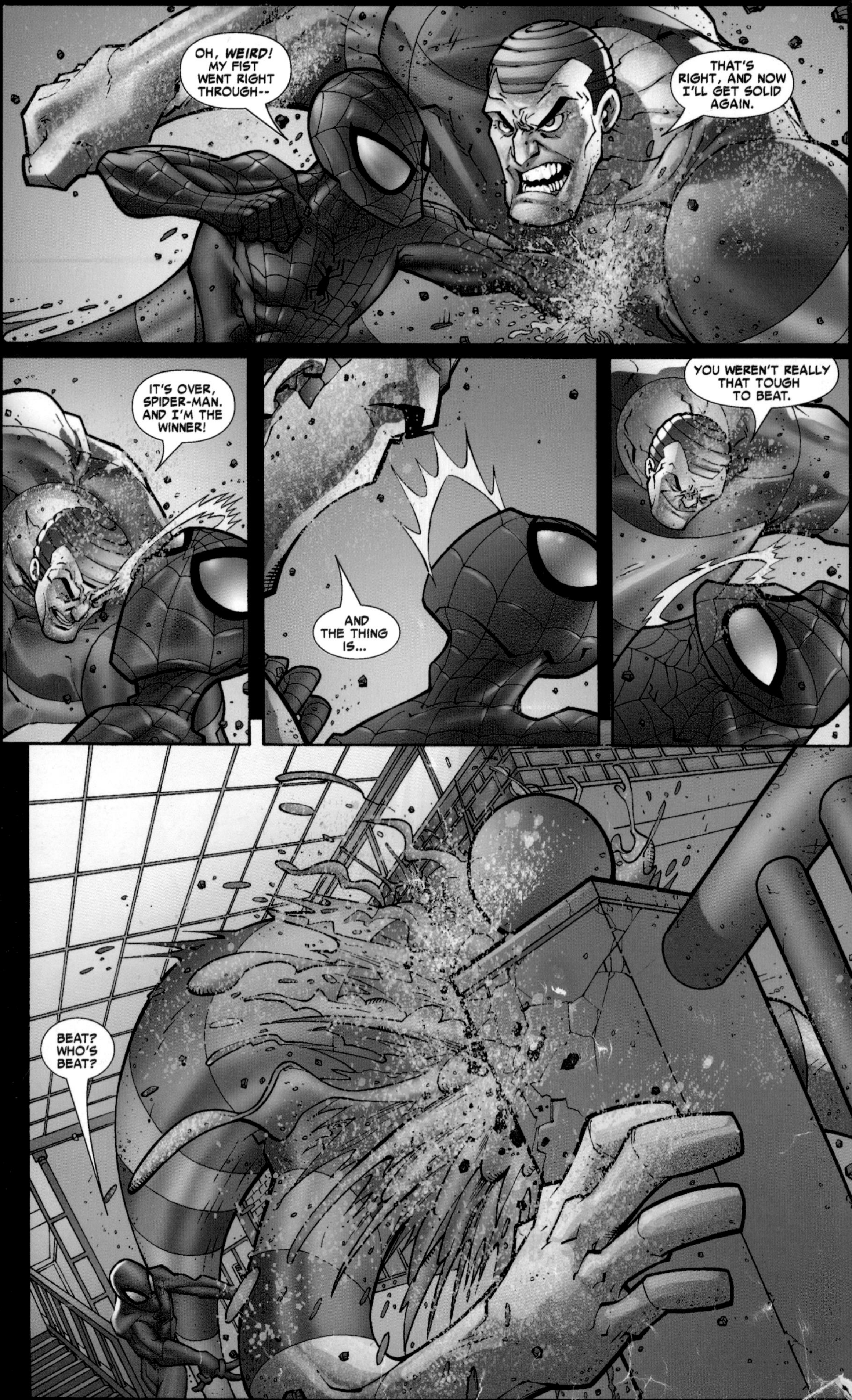
OH, WEIRD! MY FIST WENT RIGHT THROUGH--
THAT'S RIGHT, AND NOW I'LL GET SOLID AGAIN.
IT'S OVER, SPIDER-MAN. AND I'M THE WINNER!
AND THE THING IS...
YOU WEREN'T REALLY THAT TOUGH TO BEAT.
BEAT? WHO'S BEAT?

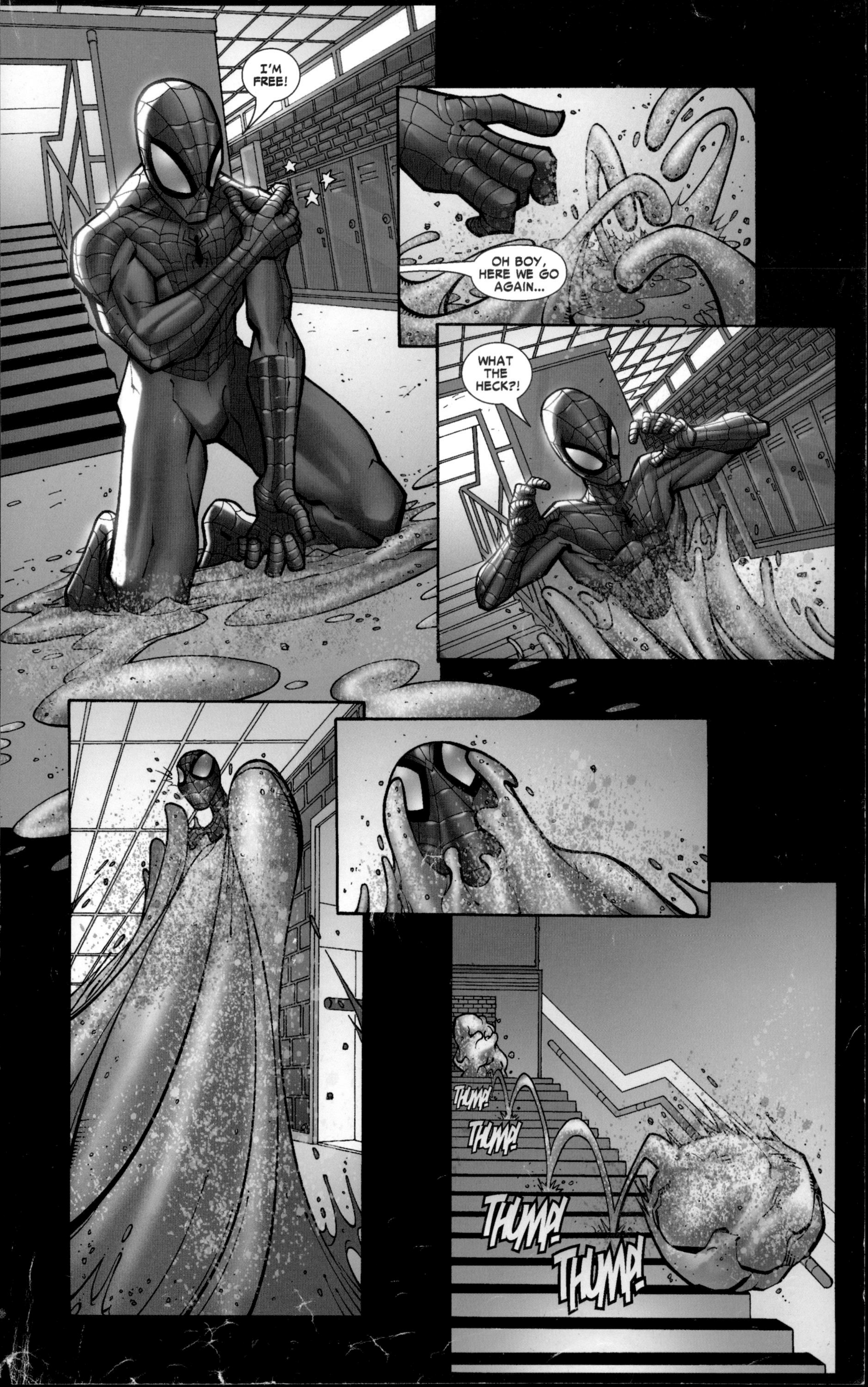
I'M FREE!
OH BOY, HERE WE GO AGAIN...
WHAT THE HECK?!
THUMP!
THUMP!
THUMP!
THUMP!

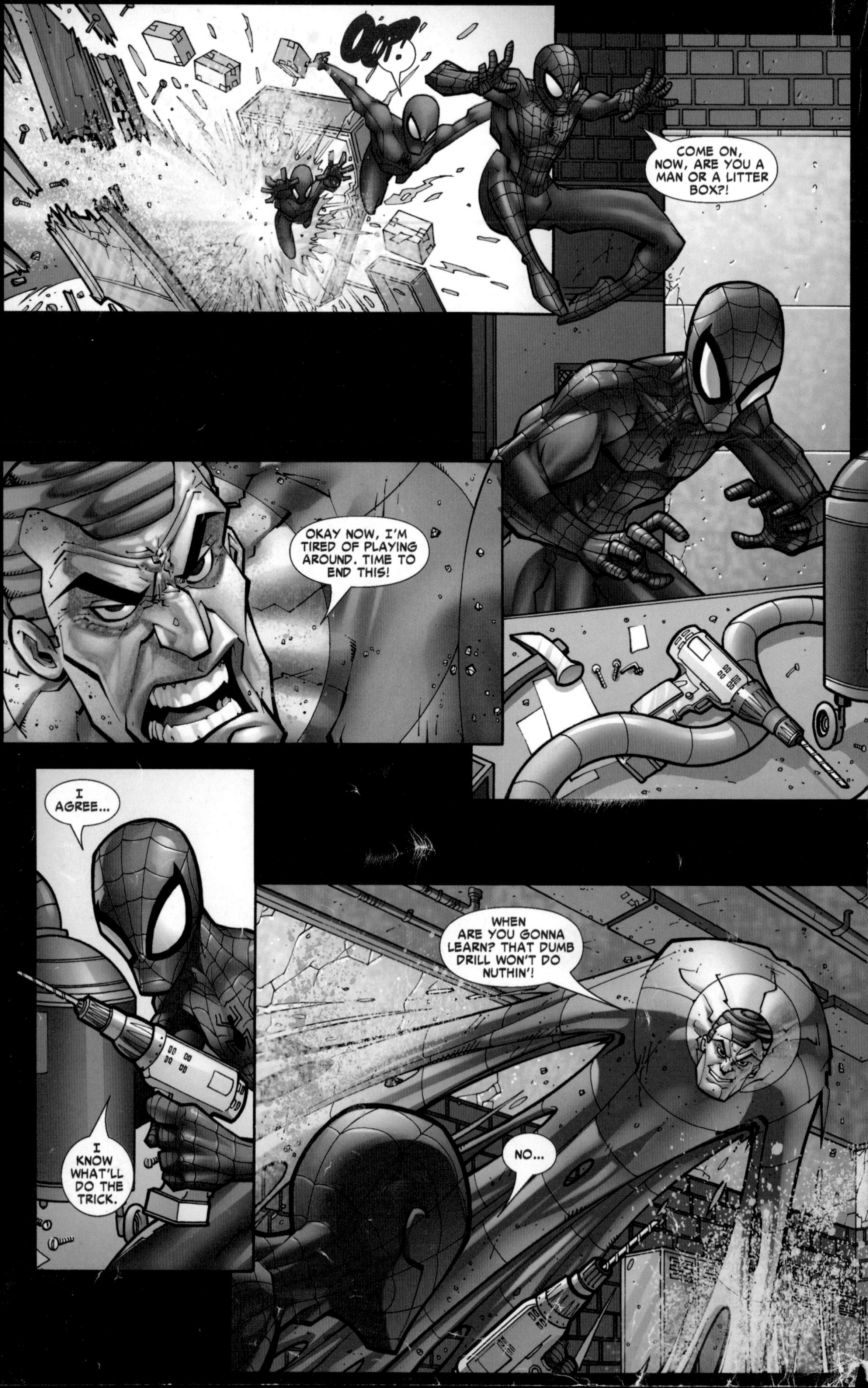
OOF!
COME ON, NOW, ARE YOU A MAN OR A LITTER BOX?!
OKAY NOW, I'M TIRED OF PLAYING AROUND. TIME TO END THIS!
I AGREE...
I KNOW WHAT'LL DO THE TRICK.
WHEN ARE YOU GONNA LEARN? THAT DUMB DRILL WON'T DO NUTHIN'!
NO...

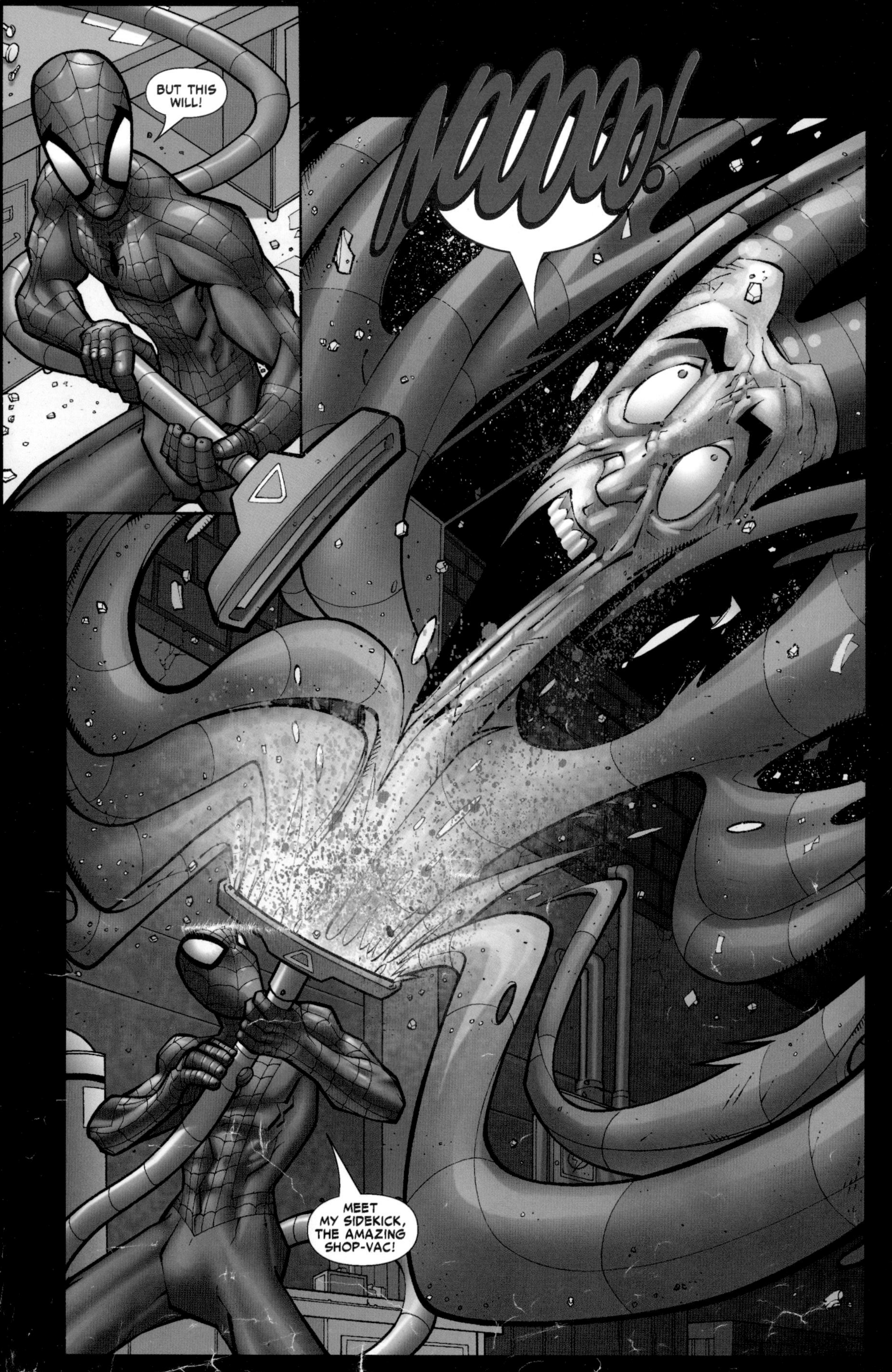
BUT THIS WILL!
NOOOO!
MEET MY SIDEKICK, THE AMAZING SHOP-VAC!

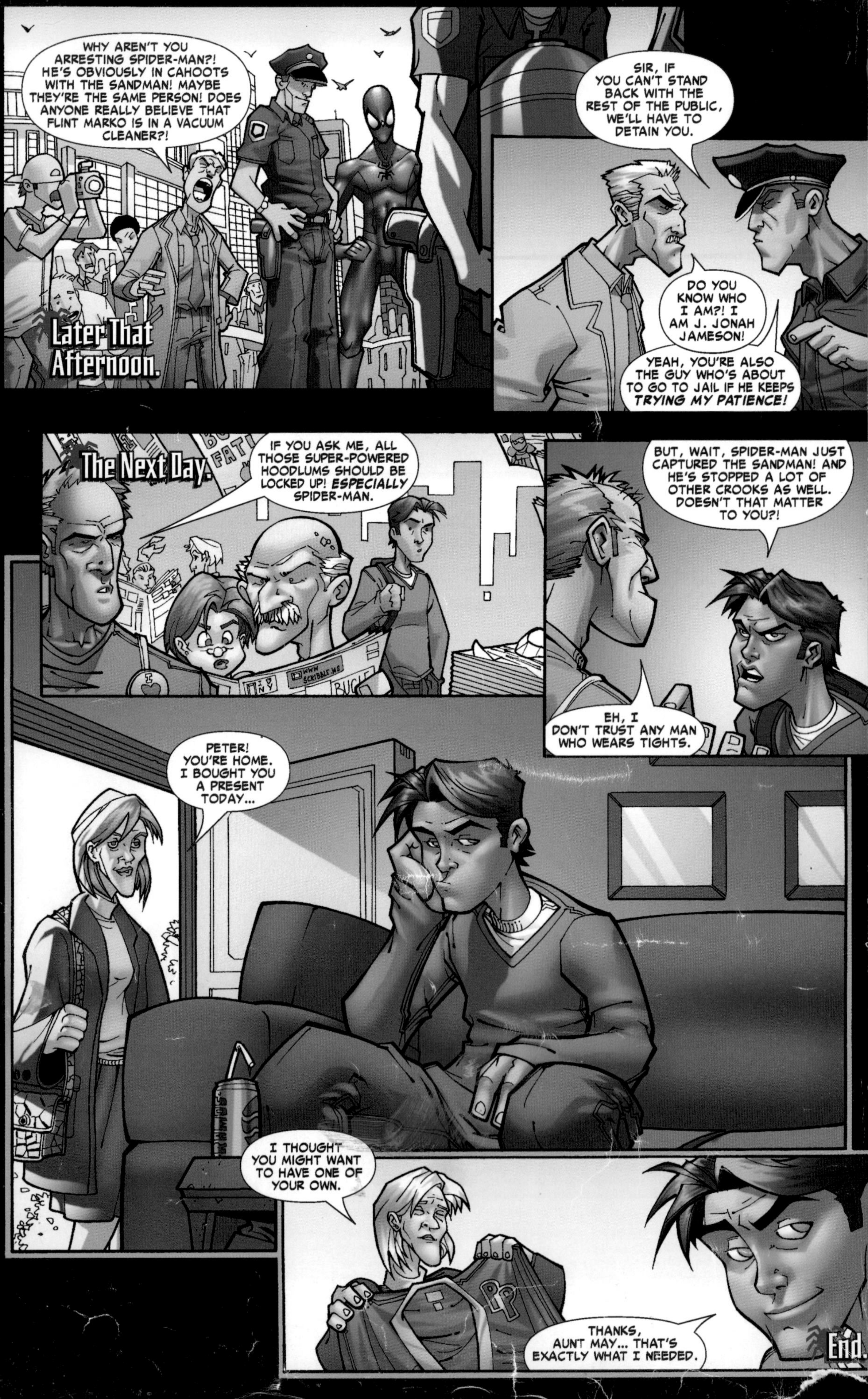
WHY AREN'T YOU ARRESTING SPIDER-MAN?! HE'S OBVIOUSLY IN CAHOOTS WITH THE SANDMAN! MAYBE THEY'RE THE SAME PERSON! DOES ANYONE REALLY BELIEVE THAT FLINT MARKO IS IN A VACUUM CLEANER?!
Later That Afternoon.
SIR, IF YOU CAN'T STAND BACK WITH THE REST OF THE PUBLIC, WE'LL HAVE TO DETAIN YOU.
DO YOU KNOW WHO I AM?! I AM J. JONAH JAMESON!
YEAH, YOU'RE ALSO THE GUY WHO'S ABOUT TO GO TO JAIL IF HE KEEPS *TRYING MY PATIENCE!*
The Next Day.
IF YOU ASK ME, ALL THOSE SUPER-POWERED HOODLUMS SHOULD BE LOCKED UP! *ESPECIALLY* SPIDER-MAN.
BUT, WAIT, SPIDER-MAN JUST CAPTURED THE SANDMAN! AND HE'S STOPPED A LOT OF OTHER CROOKS AS WELL. DOESN'T THAT MATTER TO YOU?!
EH, I DON'T TRUST ANY MAN WHO WEARS TIGHTS.
PETER! YOU'RE HOME. I BOUGHT YOU A PRESENT TODAY...
I THOUGHT YOU MIGHT WANT TO HAVE ONE OF YOUR OWN.
THANKS, AUNT MAY... THAT'S EXACTLY WHAT I NEEDED.
End.